THREESOME EROTIC ROMANCE

DISPLACEMENT

"You both need me for you to have a relationship. I'm at the center of it: I'm there because I'm not there. If I were really there, you two would not be together."

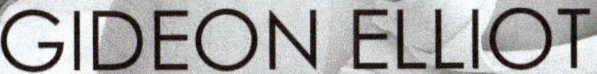

GIDEON ELLIOT

WARNING

This book contains sexually explicit scenes and adult language. It may be considered offensive to some readers. This book is for sale to adults ONLY.

Please store your files wisely where they cannot be accessed by underage readers.

* * * * * * * * * * * * * * * * * * *

About the Publisher

4Fun Publishing, a member of **BLVNP Incorporated**, 340 S. Lemon #6200, Walnut CA 91789, info@blvnp.com / legal@blvnp.com

NOTE: Due to the highly emotional reaction of some people to works of erotic fiction, any email sent to the above address that contains foul language or religious references is automatically deleted by our anti-spam software and will not be seen. All other communications are welcome.

DISCLAIMER

Please don't be stupid and kill yourself. This book is a work of FICTION. Do not try any new sexual practice that you find in this book. It is fiction and not to be confused with reality. Neither the author nor the publisher or its associates assume any responsibility for any loss, injury, death or legal consequences resulting from acting on the contents in this book. Every character in this book is over 18 years of age. The author's opinions are not to be construed as the opinions of the publisher. The material in this book is for entertainment purposes ONLY. Enjoy.

Displacement
Threesome Erotic Romance

By: Gideon Elliot

© **Gideon Elliot 2015**
ISBN: 978-1-62761-468-9

Chapter 1

It was a gray Manhattan morning. Gideon Lewis spent it among the disaffected and the bohemian. He had cut ties with family five years before. Now, he got his community and a sense of his own identity by living in a way that he sensed sabotages the orderly working of the social machinery and that is, consequently, even if un-admittedly, alluring to many people trapped, even if willingly, in that mechanism. Most people lived lives, as far as he could see, that made them dependent upon life-stifling routines, routines they adhered to for the sake of life and livelihood. Most people, he observed, were not as free as he was. They could only dream of being so, now and then. They were holding on to their vitiated lives for dear life.

He sat with a book, but he had trouble focusing his attention on it. A large cup of coffee he was unable to swallow and a croissant he had hardly touched were pushed to the side of the table. He was outside, at a café, under an awning. A light drizzle had begun. The awning outside the Riviera stretched along the sidewalk its whole length, about half the block on Seventh Avenue, across from Sheridan Square Park.

He had slept badly, had dreamed of a girl he thought he no longer desired. In the dream an exquisite intensity of desire, nevertheless, had arisen in him. The edges of fulfillment were pressing against him just as the girl slipped momentarily away leaving a promising smile behind to attest that she would hardly be away for a minute. But immediately he knew that where she had been present so palpably, now was a volume of dreamy air aching with a wish that was losing its form. No one would return. Need would remain. He awoke with a renewed sense of how alone he was.

The lingering effect, once he was awake -- perhaps this is strange -- of this awareness of loneness was not oppressive. It was liberating. Being alone -- loneliness -- took on the lineaments of exile; exile, as

Gideon was experiencing it, was an essential, ecstatic, even if achingly painful, condition of liberty. Exile transferred him to a difficult land. There he was free from the demands and the expectations that he had experienced as the means to enforce the imprisonment he had endured for as long as he could remember. Bondage had meant being forbidden the essential freedom of self-definition. It was, by definition, painfully, devitalizingly comfortable. He had managed to get out of it and felt he was an escapee, a refugee. He took refuge inside the world of his own consciousness, of his own longing, of his own anguish.

He looked up from the book he had taken with him and gazed at nothing. He had not been able to read it: undoubtedly, through no fault of its author's, it proved unable to hold his attention. As so often happened: he was reading something; the words lost their power to secure and direct his attention. It felt like he broke into fragments and one part of him blocked another. Words lost their meaning. They became mysterious vehicles carrying hidden suggestions of some incoherent whole. Although words hit the block that his mind had become and fell away, as they struck, they did revive apparently-dormant bends of thought within him, shooting stars, each of which he might, in the drowsiness that reading had induced in him, follow for a few illuminated seconds until they went dark, scattering in charred cinders like the fireworks that crumble after their copper gold bursting, and fall from the sky, decomposing. He remembered a lost, momentary cerebration of some over-illuminated joy that filled temporarily the nighttime globe of his mind the way the full moon filled the night sky. But, when he looked up from his book with the aim of following his own thoughts rather than the author's, blank and void, incoherent, and dry like shifting sand in the desert was his mind. Nothing of the moon's corona remained.

He shook his head and smiled a defeated smile. He was accustomed to the inanition. He was resigned to the infertility that blocked the longing he had to penetrate his consciousness and transpose his longing into art.

Art! What was it that "art" meant to him? A substitute for the actual? The memory or anticipation of lucid flesh? A hallucinatory shadow he could install in the place of substance? A dazzling array of hypnotic decorations conjured to usurp the pain at the center of a sense of emptiness that could never be transformed? A sense that there was nothing to realize? A lingering awareness of something that does not arrive, that cannot linger?

It was noon. Absorbed although he was by the expansive cloudy forms that he sought vainly to realize concretely, the only reality that was concrete was that he had to be at the club in an hour. He signaled the waiter for the check, gathered his things in the small knapsack through which he hooked his arms. He bore it on his back as a camel carries its hump or an old grizzled peddler the pack that weighs upon him as he tramps through the neighborhoods crying, "I cash clothes." He opened his umbrella against the drizzle that was becoming a rain, and caught the bus for the long ride up to Central Park.

He walked through the misty park under a turbulent sky, then, after he reached Fifth Avenue, he continued further east. The destination was a dark and cavernous space. There was a long nickel bar; there were tables; there was a dance floor. It was a palace of noise, of motion and commotion all night. It was quiet now, as if it were still asleep, and he were there as one of the attendants who performed their duties at its levée.

He shouldered through the swinging doors into the kitchen.

"I saw your play last night," Mike said, sneering and wiping beer foam from his mouth with the back of his hand. "I did not get what all the fuss was about."

He was addressing David Gill, an actor. Gill was playing Montano in the Shakespeare Festival production of Othello at The Public Theater. The nights the play was not being performed, he worked as one of the bartenders. Gill, tall, well-built, sandy-haired, self-assuredly handsome, adorned with a redheaded girlfriend who came to the club late every night and gave him a kiss, leaning against the bar, across the bar. Gill hardly looked up from the steak he was cutting and offered no response. Mike continued, unconcerned, more intent on provoking René, the dishwasher, with his critique: "It's what you'd expect from an arriviste nigger." Mike was a drunk and a bastard, but he had an Irishman's love of magniloquent phrases.

René remained impassive, perched on a stool by the empty sink, penciling corrections on a score he was composing.

Gideon sneezed. René looked up, at him.

"Bonjour, Jideon," he said, noticing him now. He pronounced it Jideon with a soft g, a j, with a lilting French Caribbean intonation. He was a musician of subtle proportions composing his Suite for Jazz Orchestra. He washed dishes at night and worked on his score wherever he was, whatever else he was doing.

Mike was not satisfied. His barb had been deflected by Gideon's entrance, which had removed René from the circle of his words. There was no reaction. René returned to his score. Gill, for his part, said nothing and went on eating the steak that Mike had prepared for him.

Gideon pursed his lips and shook his head at Mike and went to the locker where he hung his rain jacket.

After he had sponged his tables, placed the classic bistro red and white cloths on them, and put down napkins, peanuts, olives, and drink menus, he went outside and watched the light of late day dissolve into early evening's darkness, that time of falling day when the combination of dying light and dawning darkness make it particularly hard to see.

Early customers eat, but after ten or so, mostly people who want to drink and dance come in. The music gets very loud and never loses a hammering insistence and an irreducible presence. Colored lights flash from the ceiling. Everything you can see jumps all over the place.

Gideon was covering three celebrity tables, as well as the regular big-group tables where he usually had to provide half a dozen separate checks. A couple, in their early twenties, good looking, cute together, but unable, it seemed by the young man's discomfort, really to get into each other's rhythm, had ordered hamburgers and vodka sours. She was vertical. He was horizontal. They didn't dance. The guy was shy when he ordered, perhaps embarrassed. When she ordered, he shriveled. He kept his eyes down and avoided exchanging a glance with Gideon.

She, on the other hand, was blooming. She was dazzling. Her eyes spoke. Gideon wondered why she was coming on to him. It was cruel.

"You know what, kid?" Mike said when he asked for two burgers and fries, "it's late for a food order."

"Come on, Mike. What else you got to do?"

"This is the last one."

"Ok," Gideon said.

"You work so hard. You must be tired," the vivacious young woman said when Gideon brought them the food. "Why don't you sit down with us? I'm Olivia. He's Max."

"I can't do that," Gideon said laughing.

"Sure you can. We'll buy you a drink. Right, Max? Can't we buy him a drink?" she said. "Don't they let you drink with the customers?"

"I'm working," Gideon said, as he placed their order on the table.

Max looked up at Gideon and smiled shyly, man to man, hoping for understanding.

"I think I'm being rejected," Olivia said, coyly and with the hint of danger in her voice. "I don't like being rejected."

"If you need anything else," Gideon said, backing away, "let me know. I've got to stay on my feet." He winked and smiled.

Chapter 2

She woke him from sleep around eleven in the morning two days later with a telephone call.

"How the hell did you get my number?" he said, when she said who she was.

"The woman from the other night, Olivia," she said explaining.

"Huh," he said.

"At the club, with the very good looking guy, – I hope you won't get jealous because I say that – Max, who couldn't look at you."

He remembered her.

"How the hell did you get my number?"

"It wasn't hard," she said. "When I want something, I usually get it?"

"What do you want?" he said.

"I'd like to get to know you," she said. "Is that so bad?"

"Depends," he said.

"You sound so ferocious."

"Sorry," he said. "But it is unusual."

"For a girl to want to get to know you?" she said giggling.

"Why do you want to get to know me?" he said.

"Maybe because I find you so sexy," she said in a silken voice.

"What about your boyfriend?"

"He finds you sexy, too."

"I didn't mean it that way," he said, annoyed.

"But he does," she said, "and we'd really like to get to know you."

"Are you calling for him as well as for yourself?" Gideon said.

"I told you," she said, "it's even hard for him to look at you."

* * *

Gideon never worked Thursday nights. Despite reluctance that took the form of superstitious foreboding, the Thursday after the phone call, he met them. They had not come to the club in the interim. Although reluctance was one of the characteristics that defined his character, it was counterpoised by an absurd faith he cherished that something transformative, a Rilkean entelechy, a hidden soul that gives us the desire to realize a longed-for unknown, is waiting just outside the door of everyday life, waiting to be let in.

When he came to the corner of Seventh and Greenwich Avenues, they were already there, waiting in a café au lait Mini with the top down. They insisted he sit in the front and Olivia ride in the back. He resisted. They insisted. "We are your slaves today," she said. "Please," Max said, "sit in the front." Olivia pushed the front seat down and climbed into the back and pulled the seat up. "Please," Max said. When Gideon was belted in, Max placed his arm around his shoulder and smiled shyly. "I'm glad you're here. We are honored." "Honored?" Gideon said. It all made no sense.

They drove up the west side to The Cloisters. Max drove and played early Miles Davis, from Elevator to the Scaffold. At The Cloisters they sat in a medieval hall on worn stones and listened to period music. Soon, Olivia tilted her head just enough to indicate that she had had enough and wanted to go.

Over the Hudson the sun was setting russet. They rode back to lower Manhattan, keen for ravishing pleasure. Old music and nature's art whet their need. They were hungry for each other, but Gideon felt he had to keep up his guard.

As much as they made him the center of their attention, their love play excluded him until, as they nuzzled in each other's embrace in a booth in The Green Lion opposite Gideon, Olivia said, "Don't you think we're being thoughtless?"

"What do you mean?" Max said.

"We're not including Gideon."

"Does he want to be included?" Max inquired.

"Do you want to be included?" Olivia said, looking at Gideon.

Gideon let out a gasp of air and felt unable to answer. The throbbing pulse of forbidden desire was being crushed by the unyielding stubbornness of disquietude.

"I bet you do," she said.

What is intended to seduce can fail sometimes because it is so perfectly seductive, and just because it is seductive it demands resistance. Gideon's reluctance was reinforced just because it was threatened.

"I don't want to be in this game," he said.

Olivia looked at him with a face full of astonishment and resentment. "What do you mean by game?" she said, and leaning across the table she grabbed him by the neck and drew her to him and kissed him long, violently, and with real desire. He felt it.

"Does this look like a game?" she said.

He was frightened.

"It's getting late," he explained.

"You can sleep late tomorrow. Tonight you belong to us," Max said.

"Our guest or our prisoner. Which is it to be?" Olivia said.

"This is crazy."

"Our guest or our prisoner?" Max repeated.

It was enough, this show of compulsion, to allow Gideon to capitulate without assuming the responsibility for his longing to yield. It allowed him to surrender to the desire to go in the direction he was preventing himself from taking. His body broke open and was flooded with desire. It was what he feared. Desire is the enemy of freedom. It makes one vulnerable. The free are invulnerable and want nothing.

"I was wounded when I was in the army," Max said as Gideon's fingers felt the cicatrix on his otherwise flawless chest. Max had unbuttoned his shirt to show him. "Feel it," he said.

"You were in the army?

"I joined a few months before my eighteenth birthday."

"How were you wounded?"

"It was in a bar fight, not in combat."

"Olivia said you were shy."

"Olivia says a lot of things."

"What do you mean I say a lot of things? You can hardly speak and you blush and get embarrassed at the slightest twinge of desire. Don't frown. It's true. I love it about you. And then, you were drunk."

Max frowned.

"Stop that. It's true. I can bring you to your knees," Olivia said. "You can pretend it's not true when you're not with me, but you know it is the way it really is and that I can see right through you."

Max shrugged and smiled. "The proof of the pudding," he said.

Their unfailing wittiness mitigated the anxiety that their precocious advances caused Gideon to feel. He had undergone a transition from reluctance to eagerness. Outside, the night air was cold. The anticipation of snow was folded into the air and seemed to turn the air inside out.

And then everything stopped. Max's phone rang.

"Yeah," he said buoyantly, still high and eager in anticipation, but without a moment's passing, his expression became serious and he said, "Yes," and snapped the phone shut. He glanced at Olivia and she understood him.

"We better take you home," he said. "Tonight is not a good time."

Gideon was puzzled, of course, taken up and then dropped.

"What's the matter?"

"There's nothing the matter. We all need to get some sleep." They left it at that, refusing to say any more. Silence that Gideon did not have the audacity to break with unwanted prodding smothered their last moments together.

"Sorry about this," Max said, reaching over him and opening the passenger door for him. "Another time."

Gideon nodded. He felt his reluctance had been prescient. He also understood that he was weak enough give in to temptation. But to be seduced and abandoned before anything even happened! One had to take care that that did not happen. It meant having to be suspicious: Gideon was disturbed that he was, just by his nature, suspicious, but he was unable to risk the vulnerability and possible hurt that can come from not being wary of others.

Chapter 3

Noon the next day – he had risen from bed not a half hour earlier – Max called him.

"Sorry about last night. It was unavoidable. We really want to see you again."

"You think so?" Gideon said.

"Definitely," Max said. "I think you're very attractive."

"You are starting that again?

"Are you angry...about last night?"

"Let's say I'm confused."

"About what?

"About what!"

"Yeah."

"About how you guys went this way and that."

"We didn't go `this way and that.' Something came up that made it impossible. But we did not change what we want. Maybe you're confused about what you want."

Max sounded sympathetic. He was not scolding, challenging, or shifting blame. Gideon said, "Maybe I am."

"It's not as bad as that," Max said.

"Maybe it is."

"When can we get together?" Max answered, ignoring what Gideon had just said. "How `bout when you get off work tonight?"

* * *

Gideon was born in New York City, in the Bronx, he told them that night when they took him back to their apartment on Ninth Street. He was sent, at the age of five, to an all-day Jewish parochial school (a yeshiva) a mysterious bus ride away from his home. He went first to an all-boys yeshiva in the Bronx across from a park ending in a steep rock face, and then, until the eighth grade, to a coed one in Queens, when his family moved there to get away from the Bronx. Its effect on him, that early religious education -- quite quickly -- when he was still only five or six, was to make him realize that such religion as it represented, the behavior and rules that it imposed, were not what he was about, not at all. It was a religion of tears, of separation, of boredom, of constraint. Nor was any other religion alluring. God was a frightening specter, usurpatious and vague, contingent as something he wanted nothing to do with, something he would rather ignore, something that had, really, despite how it was pressed upon him, nothing to do with him.

He was queer before he consciously knew there was sex or eroticism. He knew eroticism before he knew sexuality. He had felt, he had imagined, the desire to surrender, to bend before a superior terror that drew him to it and bent him.

He was a stranger to himself in the world outside himself, the world that encountered him, that impinged upon him. In the world inside himself, his world alone, he was as removed from that one, too, as alien to himself as he was to the world around him. Inside, the inner world was a place of happiness or of misery, of pain or release, contingent upon influence. In the inner world, pleasures lived that were in hiding when he was awake.

He was queer before being queer had anything to do with object choice. He never experienced desire arising easily, freely, not secretly, not clandestinely, from within him, without fright. He did not meet the world with desire. His own sensations were the objects of his desire. He became the object of his own desire and he was always unattainable. Attraction assaulted him with seductive power that was mysterious; because its power was a mystery, it was absolute. His hidden desires shamed him. They took him over. But he could not surrender to them. He imprisoned them and freed them only when he could. He lived apart from the life he lived and became the slave of wishes he imprisoned. He could not get away from these imprisoned longings. He felt his will as an alien force that had commandeered him. He could not dominate his will; it dominated him. He felt his sinews stretch to high tension. It was a frightening pleasure to be drawn to where he did not want to go. Images took on kinetic power. There were negative images, too. He did not feel like he chose the objects of his fascination; they chose him – they lurked in stories he read or watched at the movies -- and he was often guilty or ashamed that he felt compelled to gaze in their direction, but that did not lessen his desire -- only made it darker, made him try to bury it deeper, made him more inauthentic at the surface.

His teachers were cruel. They encountered his neediness with mockery, and sometimes they were brutal, allowing themselves to become violent, using fists, fingers, yardsticks, and canes, punching, slapping, pinching, and beating. Some of the English teachers, in the early grades, sometimes were momentarily tender -- but not much -- and any generosity was inside their ideological/ethnic universe, from which he excluded himself -- sometimes by deliberate misbehavior, spite, and sabotage. They were kind as long as he let them shape him. The Hebrew teachers, never tender, were refugees from Eastern Europe. He was too young to understand anything about them.

He was defeated in his early, spontaneous acts of active resistance. He held back when the rabbis dragged him to class, screaming, resisting, digging in and using the weight of his five-year-old body against their tough, unrelenting hands and awesomely greater body weight. But, his active resistance was useless and caused him added anguish. That anguish accumulated within him and became his personality. His misery was the way his passive resistance showed itself. But the response his misery provoked in other people usually was rejection and anger. He received the most injury, or it seemed so to him: he was the repository of his own feelings and could not feel other people's feelings except as they impinged upon him and shaped his feelings. He could only feel his own feelings, but to feel them and to express them and to experience them as his own was impossible.

Gideon's mother, Elsa Lewis, demanded that every Friday night he go to the early evening service at the synagogue. Left to himself he would not have gone, would not even have thought of going. Going to the synagogue was one more of the compulsory things that determined his every day, things he had to do, was made to do, and had no desire to. It meant oppression, misery, tedium, and dissociation, being who he was not. Because he knew Hebrew and the inside of the religion, its prayers, obligations, and practices, the rabbi asked him to sit on the platform, an honor that he scorned and sabotaged, becoming his own victim. He sat on the platform at whose center was the Ark of the Covenant, within which were stored the sanctified Torah scrolls. With one leg crossed over his knee, he sat with a hand on his shoe. The disrespect was brazen and impossible not to notice. The rabbi wondered at this act of insolence. He understood it was a deliberate taunt. At the second service, later that evening, he spoke quietly with Gideon's mother about him, mixing tender solicitude for her and concerned reproach for the boy, compassionating her problem and warning of what might be some troubling tendencies in the boy. He explained, half apologetically, half reproachfully, that he was equally concerned that the early service, attended by the old men, should not be disturbed by some distraction from worship.

"When the rabbi reported my behavior to my mother," Gideon said, sipping on the vodka and lime Olivia had mixed for him, "she was embarrassed."

"I'm embarrassed," Gideon said then, "talking like this to you. It can't be what you expected."

"We like you?" Max said.

"I'm confused," Gideon said.

"Why are you so unsure of yourself?" Olivia said.

Gideon did not think that he was unsure of himself and the question stymied him. He was sure that a cautionary attitude to irregular occurrences like the advent of Max and Olivia was judicious and necessary. A looming sense of a hovering, incipient danger informed his action at all times. But it created a nervous need in him to fill any silence.

"My mother was not concerned that my behavior could be signaling some deep agony or that it could be a cry for her to recognize who I really was. She was concerned about the way it made her look. It was a very fucked up and self-defeating form of rebellion I had undertaken. I wanted her to stop trying to make me somebody she wanted me to be but I just was not. But I didn't believe in my right to resist, or, actually, to exist, so I did it in such a way that my act of rebellion sabotaged itself. I became a problem instead of a person. This is so trite as I tell it, but when I lived through it, it was indelible. My mother was embarrassed in front of the rabbi. With me she was angry.

She was angry because I had embarrassed her by not behaving as I ought to have behaved, as she wanted me to, for her sake. I accepted that, that I was a fault, that I was not as I ought to have been." Gideon said "I was a fault," not "I was at fault."

By the time Gideon got to be a young man he had constructed his identity out of his defeats. He did not feel, however, like the architect of that identity; it seemed to him to be the building he was born into. What was his identity? It was a work of alienation: from the religion in which he was raised, from all religious regimentation, from his own family, from those aspects of himself that longed for the warmth of family, from belief in the sanctity and the correctness of the country that demanded his heartfelt allegiance. The greatest act of alienation that he accomplished was alienation from himself. But he was not aware of it. In fact, he always sensed, with confidence that might be tried but never overthrown, that he was adhering to himself with an existential loyalty that was impervious to outside attack. He traded self-knowledge for a self-reflexive persona that was sometimes comic and sometimes desperate.

Chapter 4

In the third grade -- inside the classroom: against its windows grey mornings pressed themselves helplessly; he was seven -- they were, one morning, reading a section from genesis, in the original Hebrew. Mrs. Wall called on him to translate. "Mrs. Wall!" Dickens could not have named her better, for she embodied, was an allegorical representation of, the wall against which he banged his head forever after.

He was seven years old. She called on him to translate a section in Genesis, the passage where Jacob cooks porridge and then sells it to his brother Esau, the ravenous hunter returned from the hunt with nothing to exchange with his brother for the food he begged of him but his birthright. She had to help him find the place, and then the Hebrew words huddled before him alien and mysterious.

"You are asleep; you don't pay attention?" Mrs. Wall interrupted the hesitant reading. "You waste your time," she scolded, "looking out the window. You do nothing here. You don't pay attention. You can't learn. You won't let yourself. You are making yourself stupid. This is not what your mother sends you here for. You must be ashamed of yourself."

Her manner, her words, everything about her infuriated him. He felt his breath accumulate in his chest. It became unable to get out. It was driven back by a chokehold. And then the hold broke.

"I hate you," the words exploded as he challenged in defiant rage.

She shook her head angry with pity and impelled by a duty to work her will. She had to assert, to gain, mastery. "I will speak to you during recess," she said. "Come to my desk then. Now read the passage and translate it."

He stumbled and even before he was able to straighten up and read the next Hebrew word, she had called on someone else to do the passage and left him collapsed in his seat and gnawed by anxiety.

"Why did you say you hate me," she admonished him with the question as he stood beside her desk warding off shame.

"Because I do," he said.

"No," she answered. "You don't hate me. You hate yourself."

"I don't hate myself," he said, striking back at her. "I love myself."

"No you don't," she corrected him. "You hate yourself because you are the way you are."

"When I got older, there was no limit to the indignation I felt at her behavior. I detested her – it was no longer a matter of simple animal hatred unmediated by the intellect. The devious gall! To try to infect a child with self-hatred!" Gideon said.

"You have nearly spoken the night away, as they do in old books," Olivia said, dragging on a French cigarette.

"I'm sorry," Gideon said.

"It's good," Max said.

"I feel like we've gotten to know you," Olivia said with a hint of something mischievous in her voice. She dropped more ice into their three glasses and poured each a finger of vodka and poured tonic over that. She raised her glass in a toast and Gideon and Max followed. "Here's hoping your tongue tastes as good as it sounds," she said and kissed him before he knew what was happening.

"I love the taste of lime," she said. "Tell us more."

As Mrs. Wall was reproaching him, Gideon was chewing on the unwrapped end of a "Powerhouse" candy bar. And when she told him he did not hate her but that he hated himself, he cried out in defiance that it was not himself that he hated, that he loved himself and he felt the glow of the sweet and nutty milk chocolate as his surety.

What could he have meant when he said that? What did he mean by "love"? arises as a question, of course. What did "love" mean to him, to a seven year old? But as important, and the two questions cannot be unrelated, is the question, What did he mean when he used the word "myself?" What was, as he felt it, "myself?" The idea of "myself" was manifest in the struggle of "myself" to remain "mine" – his – and not to surrender, to surrender itself and belong to somebody else. Gideon did surrender. He accepted the self, as himself, that did deny the self that had called out the hate he felt, accepting that it was aberrant, and not him. He overcame himself. It was a betrayal that damned him to a life-long exile and to repeat sabotage, to the incessant rebellions his self-waged against him.

* * *

As the morning light rose over the city and darkness faded, and the air was fresh as if each morning it were new, newly awakened and cleansed, the three looked out at New York Bay. They had walked through lower Manhattan before the bustle.

"We want you to sleep with us," Olivia said.

Gideon said nothing.

She played her fingers over his chest. "With both of us," she said.

The morning sun gave way to clouds and the chill that covered the city caused what might have been rain to be snow. They were exhausted from their night awake and when they returned to Olivia and Max's place on Barrow Street, Olivia made them an aromatic imported French tea and they snuggled together under a quilt in a bed big enough for all of them and they fell asleep.

When they woke, Max turned on the bedside lamp and the deep blue evening that pressed against the windowpane turned instantly black. They looked at each other and asked, "Did anything happen this morning," and nobody could remember. They laughed at their puzzlement.

"What time is it?" Gideon asked, tilting the clock on the night table beside the bed so that he could see it.

I'll be late," he said.

"Can't you call in sick?" Olivia said.

"I have to go to work," Gideon said. "I need the money."

"You're no fun," she said. Gideon could not tell if she was teasing and just pretending to be petulant or if she really was.

"I really have to go," he said.

"Who's keeping you?

"Olivia," Max said, trying to moderate her rising anger.

"Don't be so spineless," she said.

"Look, I don't know what's going on," Gideon said.

"Nothing's going on," Olivia said. "I thought you were going."

"I am," Gideon said, buttoning his pea coat, his hand on the doorknob.

"I'm sorry," Max said.

"What are you sorry about?" Olivia said.

"Everything," Max said.

Olivia had soft, full, alluring breasts, skin that glowed, eyes like the sky in springtime, and a fierce temper. She was alluring and forbidding. As he jogged through the falling snow, across Eighth Street to the Astor Place subway station, careful to keep from slipping, Gideon felt a terrible confusion. He was not sure what had happened or if they would get in touch with him again.

When they did, it was only Max.

"Olivia has left me," he said.

"She left you," Gideon repeated.

"She's found a guru in Oregon."

"What happened?" Gideon said.

"I don't want to talk about it, especially not over the phone. I want to see you."

They went to the movies and in the dark Max took hold of Gideon's hand and began to trace his fingers across his palm.

"Do you know what that means?" he whispered as he leaned his lips near Gideon's ear. It excited Gideon and he said, "I do."

"Will you?" Max said.

"Do you want me to?"

"I do," Max said, touching his lips to the convolutions of Gideon's ear.

But when they got outside, Gideon felt bored and listless. His electric connection with his own body had snapped and when Max held him in his arms and pressed his mouth to his, leaning against a stone fence in a deserted and dark side alley, and said, "I want you in me," Gideon endured his advances instead of enjoying them. Max felt it and flared with inner anger but blamed himself for not being able to overwhelm Gideon and make him swell and resonate with need.

"What happened?" Max asked.

"I'm tired," Gideon said. "I need to be home." A great, dark, unfathomable sadness had come upon him.

Chapter 5

The sky was black and the stars in streams and swerves and lines and swirls spangled it with their pure blue white combustion.

"I'm so glad you consented to come with me," Max said, putting his arm around Gideon and pulling him to his flank. He kissed him on the neck just below the ear. Gideon smiled.

"I like to touch you," Max said.

"I like to be touched," Gideon said.

"Do you like when I touch you?" Max said, emphasizing the word "I" with a combination of self-assertion and trepidation.

"I do like it, yes," Gideon said, "and I wish I didn't."

"But I want you to. I want you to like it and to need it, to need me more than you can help yourself."

The road was a dirt road bordered by tamed forests on either side. The road sloped up slightly and turned in the distance. Once beyond the turn, they could see the dim lights of their inn.

* * *

"Why are you afraid to take me?" Max said, as they lay in bed side by side.

"I'm not afraid," Gideon said.

"You're a liar," Max said.

"That's not a fair thing to say."

"But it's true. You want me and you keep yourself away from me."

"It is true, I do want you."

"And you keep yourself away from me."

"I guess I do."

"You guess?"

"Okay, I do."

"So that doesn't show you're afraid?

"No," Gideon insisted. "It doesn't."

"Kiss me," Max said.

"I have to be in the mood."

Max touched him and saw that Gideon was soft.

"What's the matter, baby?" Max said, coaxing affection.

"I'm sorry," Gideon said. "Maybe I should not have said `yes'."

"I don't understand this," Max said. "Why are you shutting me out?"

"Go to sleep, Max," Gideon said. "It's late, and I want to hike to the lake tomorrow."

* * *

Max Davis was born in a wealthy suburb of Austin, Texas, but spent his boyhood roaming the woods that stretched out beyond the gated community where he lived. In the woods, his heart stretched to the sky and he bounded through the woods and stepped from one stone to another across innocent streams.

When he refused to sign the loyalty oath in the senior year of high school, everybody's attitude towards him changed and he was no longer, in everyone's eye, the person he had been for the past three, and, for some, eleven years.

In Boston, where he attended a small college that had propelled itself into a university, he met Olivia when they both auditioned for a production of An Enemy of The People. And they both did not make it, but they became friends and, for each other, they were the embodiment of what ripening genius must be.

Together, they moved to New York City without finishing school. Subsidized by Max's father, they rented an apartment on Hudson Street. And they began to live like artists. Max began painting and Olivia began writing poetry, not as she had before with a schoolgirl's sentimental intelligence, but with an eye on the market. Max's painting looked like cartoon surrealism. He used gray and muted monochrome tones.

But soon, they both felt blank.

"We've gone deep," he said.

"But there's deeper," she said.

"Can't you ever..." he pouted.

"Can't I ever what?" she said.

He looked at her with an intensity of gaze that filled his eyes with cloudy emotion.

"I'd like it to hear you say we've achieved something, that we accomplished real pieces of art, your poems and my paintings."

"Yes," she said.

"What do you mean, `yes'," he said.

"Yes," she said, "I know you would."

"That is so cold," he said. "Where have your feelings gone, the little tendrils you extended so that I knew you were there. We did accomplish something."

"What have you done that's original that matters?"

"What do you mean?"

"You know exactly what I mean. You jerk yourself off and think that's profound."

Max felt himself blocked at every exit, and everything he did seemed worthless, and nothing would ever lodge within and transform others.

"What are we going to do?" he said.

"Take a vacation," she said. "No work for a month."

It was then that they met Gideon.

"I feel like dancing," she said.

But when they stood outside, Max pursed his lips.

"What's the matter, now?" Olivia said. "You don't have to go in if you don't want to, but you are not going to stop me from having a good time."

It was then they sat a Gideon's table and Olivia flirted with him in her peremptory way and Max withdrew.

But when they were alone that night, Olivia said, "I know you like him, and I'll get him for you, but then I will leave you."

"I don't want you to leave me."

"I have no choice."

"What's that supposed to mean?"

She looked at him with irritation. She had passed her period of patience. He annoyed her. Having to explain herself annoyed her.

"That's enough now. You'll have what you want. Don't be greedy."

Seebold Davis called himself Tom from the first day of kindergarten, when he corrected Miss Minerty as she was introducing him to the other five-year olds.

"It's Tom," he said.

"But it says Seebold here," she said.

"That's what my parents call me, but I call myself Tom," he said.

"But Seebold is such an interesting name. What kind of name is it?"

"My name is Tom," the boy said with such quiet insistence that Miss Minerty yielded.

"Alright, Tom," Miss Minerty said. "Here we will call you Tom."

He disgraced himself in his father's eyes, seventeen years later, when he married a Jewish girl. Such was his resentment, so hurt was he that his father's loyalties were ideological -- or was it only institutional? -- rather than personal, that he never told him that in the way he and Laura brought Max up and in the general life and customs of the family as it was lived and as they were celebrated, they did not follow any Jewish traditions. Laura subsumed her identity to his. Max was raised as a Protestant, and it was in regard to Protestantism, not, as in Gideon's case, to Judaism, that he became apostate.

Max disappointed his father not by a disapproved marriage but by a passivity of will that was uncannily accompanied by a stubborn inwardness. He capitulated continually, hardly seeming to have any initiative of his own, it seemed, but his father could feel that he never gave in. Max, on the other hand, thought he did nothing but yield.

* * *

"My grandfather was a Nazi," Max said to Gideon as they left the exhibit at the Modern. It was the collection that had been labeled Degenerate and been shown in Berlin in the late 1930s until it became too big a draw.

"My father was very upset when he died. He called me all the time. I'd have to go stay with him until he regained some measure of calmness. They were attacks of remorse. You were there one night when he called me and we had to leave you." Max laughed. "You thought we were jerking your chain."

"Ugh," Gideon said.

"What?" Max said.

"I hate that expression," Gideon said making a face again.

"You are a Puritan. Olivia was right."

"Are you in touch with Olivia?"

"No, there would not be any point to it except to keep a painful sense of inadequacy alive in me," Max said.

"What does your grandfather's having been a Nazi have to do with the fact that you are passive?" Gideon asked.

"What?" Max said.

Gideon repeated the question, biting each word as he uttered it.

Max let out a groan-like sigh.

"I have wondered about that," he said. "My father killed himself a year after his father's death. He left a letter. He wrote that he was guilty as a son, and could not reconcile the warring passions of love and hate he had for his father. He wanted to caress him and to assault him, in equal measure. His rage at his father was fierce and impotent and his need for him was unquenchable."

Chapter 6

Max recalled one evening, as they rambled down Hudson Street -- coming home a little high from Benny's -- in the full moon's light; he recalled, it flashed through his mind, the after-image that had remained, disembodied from the flesh of its time, grafted onto his inherent being: his father standing in the dark kitchen, the room illuminated only by a mercuric November moon and enameled by a blue sky so black it glowed.

"What are you doing here?" he said when he sensed the boy's presence.

"Nothing," Max said, guilty at looking at his father.

"Do nothing somewhere else," his father said. "Git," his father said, throwing at him a crumb of affection with a smile and a wink, as he said it, as if including the boy in a spiritual conspiracy with him from which he actually was excluding him.

"I still long for him" Max said, "but I don't miss him. I oughtto, I know. There's something wrong with me because I don't."

"What?" said Gideon, somewhat lost.

"It's at the root of my passivity," he said.

"What is?" Gideon said with furrowing brows.

"The disconnection with my father?" Max said.

"It was because he was cruel to you," Gideon said, as if trying to make a child see reason.

"But he went through it himself. It was what he knew, what he was made to be."

Gideon became intrigued and wanted to write Max's history.

"It will be like sitting for me if I were a painter or sculptor."

"You want to capture my likeness," Max laughed.

"I want capture your likeness," Gideon repeated, agreeing, delighted to say it, to assert it as a fact, as a project to be undertaken.

Gideon reached over and kissed him. He felt Max yield to him like an inrush of air.

* * *

Olivia rattled the doorknob. The door stayed firmly fastened against her shaking and would not open. She wanted to call, "Let me out. Richard! Open the goddam door." She did not. She feared that if she did, she would not be able to stop and would consume herself in panic rage and humiliation.

The wind howled outside and the others who were in the house held her in their minds only to the extent that they were excited that someone was undergoing the cathartic, de-cathexis process. She was probably still passing through the first stages. Those were difficult: your past clung to you demanding your fidelity. It clung until you came to the abyss and understood in your breath that there was no birth without death. They had all gone through it and they had come out of it knowing it was one of the essential things.

Richard was in the kitchen, baking bread, his bony fingers turning and kneading the firm and subtle twist of dough that he had twice punched down and was now dividing, and laying out on tins, and shaping into loaves for the weekend.

He frowned when Marc walked in.

"I was mistaken," Marc said

"You want to be the boss," Richard said.

"I'm sorry," Marc said.

"You think of me as the boss, and you're jealous."

"What can I do?"

"Purge yourself of envy."

Olivia stopped rattling the handle when she was convinced the door would not budge and that no one would come save her from this confinement. She had heard of it, but she thought she would evade it. Richard had made her feel special, and she had slept beside him for more than a week until tonight when she was surprised by his command that she should undergo the de-cathexis.

"Don't do that to me, Richard."

"Why not? Do you think you're special because I take you to my bed? I take everyone to my bed."

Olivia lay on the wooden bench inside the locked cell tearing herself apart to see if she felt that she was special. But she had trouble understanding what the word "special" meant. She could not focus on where she could search or what she was supposed to look for. She strayed among thoughts of regret and desire; she was savaged by feelings of frustration and rage.

In the morning she had no greater understanding of the world than she had the night before, nor had the pain that had taken her by surprise when she fell from favor become any less now than it was then. But it did not matter. The tempos of her every function had been slowed down. She felt that she had time to breathe; as she followed her breath she lost awareness of her mind; whatever it was she was thinking became a blank. She looked at how she had become, as if from a great distance, and was quietly fascinated. She was a spectator, as removed as a spectator, at her own transformation.

Richard was pleased when he saw her. She knew he was. It irritated her. He smiled, wrinkled his cheeks tilted his head to one side like a bird and spoke through playfully clenched teeth.

"It is morning," he said. "We should have breakfast."

"I'm not hungry."

"Petulant," Richard said.

"Call it what you will," Olivia said. "I thought we were here for Enlightenment, not abuse."

"How can you tell the difference between the two?"

"Don't head fuck me," Olivia said, and slapped him.

Richard backed away, touching his fingers to his cheek.

"How's that for enlightenment?" Olivia said.

"The baby beats the nurse."

"I want my things."

"The enlightened spirit does not require or desire things."

"But I want mine."

"You pledged them to the group."

"I have changed my mind."

"No, you haven't. It's the same mind you came here with. Your mind is as bound and hobbled as it was when you came here," Richard said, raising his voice. "Your mind is your prison."

"And you know all about prisons," Olivia said, in defiance.

"I see so many people who think they are free are really locked up."

"And you are free?"

Richard smiled cryptically.

* * *

Max showed Gideon the beginning of a story he was trying to write. It shocked Gideon when he read it, not because of its contents but because of what it revealed about Max, how unlike what he presented to the world; suggesting what he had kept hidden:

I am not pleased -- Gideon read -- that I long to be subservient and that I get excited by the thought of being entirely dominated and forced to surrender control to a powerful, overpowering man, but every night, as if in a trance I change into a torn and tight slutty uniform and walk the street with my eyes following the pavement as it rolls under me, waiting with needles of expectation for a voice that will hail me and stop me, take me by the arm and let me know that I will be his.

Even if I am tired or would rather stay home and read Proust, even if I know that I do not want another night of being slapped and teased, humiliated and penetrated, I still find myself checking myself out in front of the mirror and then cruising through the streets.

It was on one of those nights when I was dull of desire that Graham saw me and stopped me saying, "You are just what I want tonight."

I recognized his voice, and I nodded to him and kept my head lowered, "It's a nice evening," I said.

"Buy you a drink?" he said with a friendly smile.

"Thank you," I said, meaning the words as a refusal, but he ignored that and took me by the arm, and I let myself be led down the street to Benny's as he steered me by the arm through a crowd of losers who were watching us with envy.

We drank martinis and I felt on edge, stuck where I did not want to be.

"I'm tired tonight," I said. "I know you're not supposed to say a thing like that in a situation like this," I said, apologetically, "but I want to be honest with you. I don't know how obliging I can be tonight. I think I'd rather just go home."

Graham smiled. "You don't have to apologize," he said. "I know how to turn you on, no matter how you think you feel."

I just looked at him with a half sleepy stare.

He lifted his glass and finished his drink, and as he did, so did I.

"I need to go home," I said.

"No, you don't," he said.

We were at his place in a few minutes. He pulled me close to him as we walked there. I was oblivious to everything, as if sleepwalking.

It was warm inside. He unbuttoned my shirt. I breathed deeply as he gently played with my nipples. He continued, increasing the pressure. I felt the beginnings of a headache.

"Please don't," I said. "Not tonight. I don't want to go there."

"You will."

"Not tonight," I said.

It was as if I had not spoken.

"Are you listening?" he said.

I had not heard what he said.

"What?" I said.

He pinched my nipples harder.

I bowed my head. I was stung by his slap across my cheek.

"None of that abjection shit. I like to see pride in a submissive."

"I don't want to be a submissive."

He pinched my nipples yet harder and brought me with a jerk to my full height.

I was not proud that I was a submissive. It was a curse I could not lift.

Graham teased my lips softly with his index finger, then with that same finger, one digit stronger than my entire force of will, gently parted them and limned the crests of my teeth with the taint of desire, then pressed my jaw down, and down my open mouth drove his finger to the back of my throat, and I gagged.

I could not get rid of the feeling of being enslaved all throughout the next days when I had to have a clear mind and a ready disposition. I needed to be able to be interested in things other than myself and the reverberations of my yearning. There was a familiar feeling taking hold of me, being wary.

I could not live in both worlds, and I was not sure which one I wanted.

Gideon stopped reading and looked at Max. Max blushed.

"I told you I was taking a risk by showing it to you."

"Is that the whole thing?"

"It's very short."

"I don't understand what both worlds you're talking about."

"The worlds of assertion and of capitulation."

Gideon waited but Max said nothing more.

"What happens?"

"I don't know."

"So it's more like a picture of a psychological condition than a story set in motion by that condition or recounting the adventures of that condition."

"I never thought about it, really."

"That's hard to believe," Gideon said.

"I just try to follow my imagination. An artist makes things out of whole cloth and air."

"You really want me to think so?"

"I could not write if I didn't."

* * *

Olivia found a boy in a café in Oregon and hitched with him to northern California. She moved in with him immediately. Brandon was a software engineer. After eight years working for Apple, he had left the company soon after its founder died. A sense of loss weighed heavily upon him. He had stashed away so much during the years there during which he spent most of his life – his waking life, and sometimes he even slept on a couch in his office and had coffee in the morning in the commissariat -- that he had no need to worry about making money. He decided to purge himself of uneasy longing by undertaking a break from everything and spend two weeks in the wilderness, in an Oregon forest, with water, only, nuts, apples, and brown rice cooked over an open fire.

He breathed through his nostrils on the fifteenth day and the oxygen flooded his forehead; his eyes swooned and his sight sharpened; his spine stretched long and filled with energy. He stood and looked at the mountains. He breathed in the morning air, saw the light crash into the forest through the gate of foliage, and watched the sky from an open grove.

He walked through the woods to the highway and along the highway -- unsuccessfully -- hitching for several hours until he came to The Lost Road Café. There he saw Olivia and felt that he had been renewed. She looked at him, too, and smiled.

"Where are you headed?" he asked.

She shook her head, raised her shoulders, and smiled.

"Come with me," he said, believing that what was happening was inevitable.

She said "yes" before she asked where.

"Do you mind if I sleep somewhere else tonight?" Olivia asked as they nuzzled together under a tree in the little woods on the land that his house was built on as the declining sun made the landscape golden. She had lived with him nearly three months.

"No," Brandon said. He had been meditating on the condition of non-attachment.

Even though she remained resting in his embrace, she had disappeared. She began to feel restless from the weight of his body pressing against hers, against her. He was asleep. She freed herself from his hold and rose. It woke him.

"Where are you going?" he asked.

"To meet someone," she said.

"Now?" he said.

"I'll be away for a few days. I'm not sure how many," she answered and walked to the house.

Brandon sat up and watched her disappear.

Chapter 7

Despite Gideon's presence, there was a palpable hollow for Max where Olivia had been. He was haunted by a concrete sensation of absence. It was not even a sensation of her absence anymore. It was just a pang of pure absence. It resided in him the way feelings of joy or sorrow can, and when they do, how strongly they affect the essential disposition that envelopes a person, the disposition that makes the shadow a person casts in the world!

"But she crushed you," Gideon said. "I don't understand."

When Olivia met Max, she believed that he possessed the kind of integrity she could rely on, the kind of solidness she could build on, the kind of imagination that could restore light to a life that had fallen in shadow. She throbbed inside with energy she did not know how to use and kept spilling in misplaced and shaky enterprises.

"I want someone who can go places with me," she said, but/and Max wondered where there was to go. He listened to her, however, and usually kept silent for fear of her wrath but also, for his sense of his own inadequacies. It was not that there was no place to go, no place worth going to. It was that he was removed from the energy of any quest. Curiosity and venturesome energy had been pulled out of him, drained out of him, pressed every day out of him. She represented possibility for him, and all too often she frustrated what she offered. Had he been someone else he would have had the resources to take possession of her. But even if Olivia could not admit it, she sensed in her deepest fibers what was numb and dissatisfied in him and it sent her excitement crawling back upon her. Rather than desire, will -- equally defiant and defeated -- drove them to each other. Sometimes they really met. Often they were searching for each other; sometimes hiding from each other.

"I miss her," Max said.

"That is because you never had her," Gideon said.

When Olivia returned to Brandon after a few days he told her he could not go on that way despite thinking before it happened that he could. When she said she could not be chained, that she needed to move when and how she wanted to and that he would have to accept it and adjust to it, he said he could not, and she left him.

Olivia fell asleep on the train, in her seat, on the way to Connecticut. She dreamed that fields of eggs began to snow. She was shivering as she ran through them barefoot in her shift. "What can this mean?" she asked herself inside the dream. "I must be dreaming; that's it," she dreamed she thought. "In the waking world this is impossible."

She loved Max; she was angry at him. She had left him once it became obvious to her that he had left her first, perhaps that he had never really been there in the first place. She made sure always to protect herself: humiliation was always a possibility, and it did not turn her on.

Thinking of him now, all she could feel was his sweetness. It was not his fault that he had fallen in love with Gideon. Gideon was irresistibly needy and adorably blind when it came to himself and to most other things. His greatest wisdom was to have made the shell of a world to contain himself that he had made. But she wanted to crack Gideon's shell and get inside him.

She called him when she arrived in New York. She asked him not tell Max yet that she had returned and she told him she wanted to see him and that he should meet her in front of a certain movie theater in So-Ho, that she wanted to walk to the water with him and maybe they could take the ferry. But they only stood looking out at the water of the bay and then facing each other in a restaurant nearby.

"Why did you leave?" he asked her.

"Why is that a question for you to ask?"

"Because it injured Max."

"Not more than your ability to heal him. Which is what you wanted."

"I don't know what you are talking about."

"You won't let yourself. You both need me for you to have a relationship. I'm at the center of it: I'm there because I'm not there. If I were really there, you two would not be together. Max pours out his neediness to you and you are melted by the warmth of his unhappiness, and try to make him happy, not because you care about him but because you see yourself in him."

"What do you want?" Gideon said, feeling something unpleasant like the urge to slap her.

"You," she said, "inside me."

Gideon breathed in and widened his eyes. He became dizzy and wanted to flee, but he sat at the table. The replica of New York lampposts of a century ago dimly lighted the place; turned it into an indoor extension of the late autumn early evening outside.

"I don't feel right having this conversation without Max."

"Did it bother you just as much to talk about me with Max when I wasn't there?"

Gideon said nothing.

"Take me home," she said.

"Where do you live?"

"I'm staying at a friend's place on Perry Street while she's in Paris making a commercial for Christian Dior."

She stashed some cash into his hand as the cab pulled up in front of the place she was staying at on Perry Street saying, "Pay the driver."

"I have money," he said.

"My treat," she said, leaving the money in his hand.

Upstairs, she said, "I am not good at not getting what I want. You should know that by now. I said it in our first phone call." She approached him and put her hands flat on his chest. When her lips opened against his, forcing them open, her palm caressing the back of his neck drew him tenderly to her. To him it felt like a long-awaited gift being offered. She drew back and smiled. He moved back to her and drew her to him and now his tongue entered her mouth and she closed her lips upon it.

It was warm in her bed in the morning and he was happy.

* * *

Max was in hysterics that afternoon.

"Where were you? I tried calling you I can't tell you how many times. You never answered your phone. And that's not like you."

"Olivia is staying on Perry Street," Gideon said.

"She's back?" Max said.

"I saw her last night."

"And she didn't let me know."

"She just got back. She intends to get in touch with you."

"But she got in touch with you immediately...You...slept with her," Max said.

Gideon nodded. Max let out a breath, bit his finger, and shook his head.

"Why haven't you called me?"

Max was surprised to see her in the lobby during the intermission and walked over to her.

"Why haven't you called me?"

"Not here. Not now," Olivia said, as if gently reproaching him for bad manners.

"Don't I deserve some kind of explanation?" he nevertheless insisted, gripping at her with his need.

"I don't owe you anything," Olivia said as Miriam – but she did not introduce her to Max -- returned with two plastic champagne flutes and gave one of them to Olivia. They touched glasses and drank. Olivia had turned from him. Max stood dumbfounded and wounded. He could say nothing. Olivia had walked away from him even as she stood there, sipping champagne with a woman he did not know.

Max found it impossible to sit through the second half of Traviata and left the opera house in despair.

* * *

When Max finally knocked on Gideon's door, he had been wandering through the streets of lower Manhattan for hours, grief-stricken and tormented. When Gideon opened the door he burst into sobs and fell into his arms.

"I can't help it. I need to be with you," he said. "It's crazy. You're the last person I should have to turn to. Why did you betray me?"

Gideon held him but said nothing, feeling his anger and despair.

"Answer me, godamit," Max shouted through his tears.

"I didn't betray you. You know that."

"That's what kills me. You weren't even thinking of me. Have I a right to want you to think of me? Would it make it better? Would it make it worse?"

"You can want what you want," Gideon said.

"A lot of good it does me."

"Do you know what you want?"

"I didn't come here for this," Max said.

"What did you come here for?"

"If I've got to say it, you don't know it."

"We're separate people."

"But we don't have to be." Max let it hang at that, unable to say out loud: "We wouldn't be...if only...you gave yourself to me."

"You're weaving gossamer ropes and choking yourself with them," Gideon said, happy to be able to put it so exactly. But Max did not know what he was talking about.

* * *

"You're bored," Gideon said to Olivia.

It was nothing about Gideon, per se, she assured him. It was about herself. Anger was frozen at the center of her belly. She said it told her that she had betrayed something essential about herself. She was at a loss, she said, and that made her all the angrier – frustration made her angry.

"What the hell are you so angry about?" Gideon challenged her. Every word she said, every gesture she made was smoldering and charred. Everybody was unreliable, and it offended her, threw her off, isolated her.

"You wouldn't know even if I told you," Olivia said.

Gideon absorbed the offense without saying anything.

She stared at him. He took a step backwards, away from her. He turned and opened the door. There was a smell of coffee and toast in the hallway.

"You got what you wanted," he said. "I'm finished with this. Go back to Max. He's waiting."

"What about you?" she said. "Did you get what you wanted? Or can't you admit that you want anything."

"I got a lot," Gideon said. "But I'm not sure I want it." He turned away from her and went down the steps.

"Fucker," she cried after him.

Outside, the air was clear and crisp and palpable. He breathed and his eyes sparkled.

"I don't think I want to start this over again," Olivia said when Max called to ask to see her.

"I'm not asking for that," he said.

"Well, what are you asking for?"

"To see you," he said.

"To what end? To persuade me to do what I don't want to do?"

She had not forgotten the peace she had felt when Gideon closed her door.

"I'm sorry, Max," she said.

"No, you are not," he said and shut his phone.

She heard the call die.

"You're right," she said, after he was gone.

The End

Here is a sample from another story you may enjoy:

GIDEON ELLIOT

TABOO EROTICA

HYPNOTIZED

3 IN 1 BOXED SET

I'D KNOWN Jason since we were kids. I've always admired him – so much that it sometimes overwhelmed me. My admiration began with the way he looked. I always just enjoyed seeing him. He was a scrawny kid at the pool in the summertime, but lithe. He was adorable. When I think of him now, as I remember him during the summer, many years ago, when we were both seven, I can still see him as we undressed in the bungalow our families shared in Rockaway. He looked, stretching himself out of his little wet speedo, like nothing so much as a plucked chicken.

In his early teens he was smart and snappy and thoughtful, dressed sharp, got into gym and working out, as well as folk music – he taught himself guitar -- film noir, the Marquis de Sade, differential calculus, Nietzsche, and automobile engines. Girls talked about him, giggling with desire. He was easy around them, affectionate, cuddly, and, although he dated, he never got tied down to one girl friend. But none of the girls he dated expected him to, and none of them lacked for dates with other guys.

What was really beautiful is that he allowed me to love him. He was glad to accept it; he didn't push me away. When I looked at him with wondering eyes, with helpless admiration, he just grabbed me by the shoulder and horsed around for a minute.

Then he'd smile in the friendliest way. I didn't feel the least bit ashamed for showing my devotion. I'm always at ease with him but there are moments when I feel the excitement shaking inside me like I do with no one else. He's noticed it. And he doesn't hold it against me.

He'd go nuts if he couldn't accept love, 'cause he's a guy that everybody's crazy about, and he even can stay friends with girls who are dying for him but he won't sleep with them.

***

WE WERE in Butler library. We were seventeen. It was after ten, and the place was relatively empty. I'd managed to read all of Mill's *On Liberty* and I was thinking about the various possible extents and limits of human responsibility. I didn't get anyplace solid in my thought. I was spacey, floating, feeling like I was thinking but unable, the next moment, to remember exactly what I had been thinking.

Suddenly I heard fingers snap in front of my face and I saw Jason grinning. He'd just finished an assignment in differential calculus. If I had just had to squeeze my brain into that mold for two hours, I would not have been smiling.

"Where are you, Buddy?"

"I'm thinking about the limits of social responsibility and how you determine how much control any person can put on another; or an abstract group, like society, on the individual."

"Did anyone ever tell you that you lose yer bloom when you think."

"Cut the shit," I said, laughing at how beautifully he could move me from one place to another without even noticing it. "Aren't you tired of calculus already?" I said. "You're thinking all the time, and you haven't lost your bloom."

"Let's get some coffee," he said, throwing his arm round my shoulders.

"And stay up all night?"

"Don't worry."

Well, when Jason says "don't worry," you don't worry.

I couldn't get enough of him. I suppressed my sexual desire in order to be able to keep being with him. He didn't mind how I felt, but still I didn't want to make him uncomfortable by putting him in the awkward position of feeling like demands were being made on him, or of seeming like he was rejecting me. Most of the time it worked. I forgot about how much I wanted him and just enjoyed being with him the way we were. I forgot my sexual desire, or maybe it lingered as a ground bass giving greater resonance to whatever we did. I had become like an anorexic. Something else was more important to me than eating.

If you enjoyed this sample then look for **Hypnotized**.

Also by this Author

A Second Chance

The Recruiter

A Furtive and Hidden Embrace

Diamond Shadows

Displacement

Keen Obedience

Between Two Thieves

Heart's Desire

Sensual Surrender

Erotic Aggression

Don't Forget You Love Me

Unstable Emotion

The Hazard Game

A Knight in the Forest

Captured Emotions

The Mesmerist's Tale

On His Own

The Good Bitch

Succumb Touch

Blue Identity

***

I REALLY LOVE Reviews!

If you enjoyed this book, please share the love and don't forget to leave a review on Amazon or the site of any other retailer you purchased this book from!

I highly appreciate your reviews, and it only takes a minute to write & post one. I can't tell you how much this means to me!

You'll find the list of all my books on my Author Central page... just in case you'd like to leave a review for other books of mine you've read but didn't have time to leave a review.

*Amazon Author Central – http://www.amazon.com/Gideon-Elliot/e/B00DUYBEQC

One Last Thing, For Kindle Readers...

When you turn the page, Kindle will give you the opportunity to rate this book and share your thoughts on Facebook and Twitter. If you enjoyed my writings, would you please take a few seconds to let your friends know about it? Because... when they enjoy they will be grateful to you and so will I.

Thank You!

Gideon Elliot
gideon_elliot@awesomeauthors.org

About the Author

Gideon Elliot was born in 1981 in Wichita, Kansas.

He grew up in San Francisco and spends the greater part of the year, now, on one of the Cyclades Islands in Greece where he runs a jazz café, paints, writes poetry, and swims.

He has a small apartment in Greenwich Village, where he stays from the middle of November to the end of April and, during those months, manages an erotic men's clothing shop. He began writing erotic fiction at the age of fifteen.

You may also like the books by these authors:

AMY REDEK

THE WIZARD OF KOS

Bisexual Erotica

Sexy, Magical, Fantasy

Milos Drake was and had been a wizard for the past sixty years and came from a family of wizards that had always lived in the village of Hazelwood. He was young for his age for the average life of the wizards in the village was four hundred years, give or take a few decades. Unless, like in the case of his parents, some unforeseen accident occurs like trying a new spell to transport themselves to another village. Something went wrong and they were never seen again.

That had happened twenty years earlier, and ever since, the other wizards of the village had worked on this and finally made a success of it, but though many of them travelled the length and breadth of the country, they never found the parents of Milos. So at the tender age of forty, he became an orphan and lived alone with just his inside and outside elves. As it implies, the inside elf look after everything inside of the house while the outside elf saw to the garden, vegetable patch and the upkeep of the outside of the house.

The inside elf wore an orange smock while the outside elf wore a green one. The colours never varied and they were known respectively as Quirk and Quarrel. They were aptly named for Quirk, the inside elf had the tendency to never put things back in their right places and a habit of mishearing whatever order he was given.

Quarrel, the outside elf would nearly always pick an argument with Quirk when a specific vegetable was required. He hadn't planted them yet; they were not yet fully grown; they'd been eaten by fly pests, whatever. He was always trying to pick an argument with Quirk who had become wise to him and would ask for things like turquip beans or fantail radishes just to set him off.

In spite of the hassles those two had together, Milos was well looked after and never ever really wanted anything else, except the one thing that any young man desired, and that was the company of a female.

Now you might say that sixty years of age was getting a bit past the time of wanting a young woman but you must realise that they lived for nearly four hundred years and so by any human standards of life, he was only just reaching his prime.

Besides, they didn't normally marry until they were a hundred years old as a rule and even then, the village kept control over the birth rate to maintain a steady flow of growing wizards so as not to exceed the number that could be contained within the village.

There were three other young male wizards of his age and four female ones, and when he reached the age of ninety, he was expected to start courting one of these females with the intention of marriage and continuing the life of the village.

But he had not been under any parental control for the past twenty years and so began to take liberties as far as the women folk of the village were concerned. He was a handsome man and looked quite virile and had a likeable charm about him that soon had woman falling over themselves for him. The best part for him was that he didn't have to use any magical incantations or things like that, it was just his own charm that wooed them to become like putty in his hands.

He knew the theory of having sex with a woman but had not as such been able to get onto the practical side until he came across Lilith Buckfaster. She was a buxom girl of his own age and they had attended wizard school together as had the other three girls and boys of their age. She was one of the four girls that he would be expected to be married to when the time came, but he was too anxious to wait that long.

He found her out in one of the surrounding meadows one fine day, searching through the grass.

'Hello Lilith, what are you looking for?' he asked, walking over to where she was moving the grass about with a stick.

'I'm looking for some worzel fungus for a potion I'm making,' she replied, bending down as she looked at the ground. He could see her firm breasts inside the bodice she was wearing and felt himself start to stir at the sight.

If you enjoyed this sample then look for **The Wizard of Kos**.

ANGUS MacGREGOR

RESCUED

HOT ROMANCE EROTICA

THE PARDONED SERIES, BOOK 2

She giggled to herself remembering when she was younger, just really beginning to be curious about boys. One night when Jack had been complaining of allergies, she had intentionally given him way too much Benadryl which knocked him out. She waited until the house was dark and still, and sneaked into his room, pulled back the covers, and cautiously slid his underwear down. She stared at his penis, now large and man-sized, framed with soft brown curls, as it hardened in the cool air and soon lay back against his soft belly. She had no sexual attraction to Jack, but part of her wanted to hold his dick and just see what it felt like. She had the distinct feeling that he wouldn't have minded. She finally stretched out her hand and held the heavy shaft and marveled at how soft and hard it was at the same time stroking the shaft up and down until he was rock hard and a clear drop of pre-cum oozed from the tip. She had thrown the covers back over him and ran to her room, embarrassed and aroused at the same time. As she lie in the quiet of her own bed, she slid her hand down between her legs and rubbed her clit as images of Jack were replaced with Charlie Morris, a handsome boy from her Algebra II class. He sat beside her, and Cassie had noticed that he was constantly adjusting his dick in class. Often when he was asked to go to the whiteboard to work a problem, his erection pressed hard against his jeans revealing a thick round head. She imaged her hand sliding up and down his hard cock, lowering her head to his lap, feeling the heat of his member in her hand and against her face as she brought herself to a shattering climax.

Cassie grinned thinking how much Jack would love that story and would give her hell for being such a perv. He would offer to show her the real thing again any time she wanted, she figured. Her little sister Carly was sweet but interestingly, Cassie didn't feel nearly as close to her. The two of them had hardly ever spoken about boys and sex, whereas she and Jack were always bouncing their exploits off each other. Of course in her case, they were so few she didn't bother saying too much. Jack, on the other hand, enjoyed being as shockingly graphic with her as he could be, but a big part of her enjoyed the playful, dirty talk.

Cassie had a few close calls in high school. The most intense was with Charlie Morris, who had asked her to prom when she was a junior.

The two had spent a few fun hours on her bed or his when their families weren't around. The week before prom, he had pulled his dick out, and she finally got to really touch it. He pushed his jeans and shorts down to his ankles and pulled his shirt up to his neck. She knew he wanted her to suck it, but she wasn't sure about that. As she stroked his penis, he softly stroked the lips of her vagina and teased with the opening, which was wet and wanting. She gasped as his finger slid gently inside her as they kissed. Her hand sped up stroking his cock until he groaned. She watched as thick pearly ropes of semen blasted on his firm belly and got caught in the soft light brown hairs that ran from his navel to his groin.

After prom, the two had driven to a logging landing out on Baber Mountain. The night had been warm for May. Cassie had smiled when she saw the planning Charlie had done to for the night. He made a comfy place on the back of his pickup bed. The two sipped some lemon-flavored vodka, which was horrible, and lay with their formal clothes while they kissed and groped each other.

Cassie remembered his penis straining against the thin fabric of the tuxedo pants...

If you enjoyed this sample then look for **Rescued**.

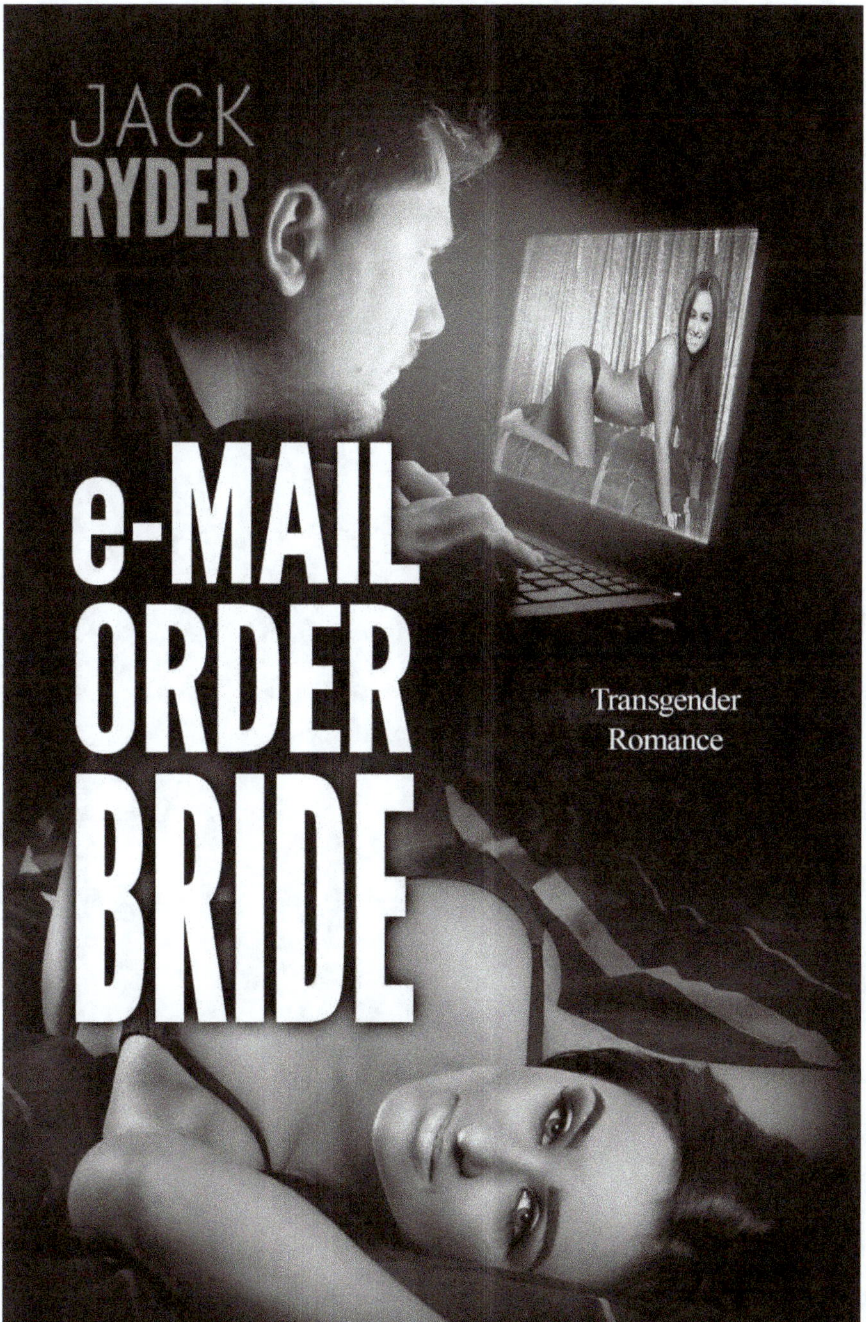
JACK
RYDER
e-MAIL
ORDER
BRIDE
Transgender
Romance

Seatac was a mad house at 9pm on a Friday night. I was glad that I had left early so I had plenty of time to deal with the sports traffic on I-5 due to the Mariners Game. Then I had to deal with the security checks to make my way to the proper air terminal gate for Sam's arrival. I made it to the gate with ten minutes to spare. I felt an overwhelming giddiness as I watched her airplane pull up to the loading dock.

"Ooooh, Fuck me," I gasped beneath my breath as I saw her coming down the ramp. She was wearing a white tube dress that fit her like a second skin. It was so short that I could see the bottom inch of her white panties as she walked towards me. She was wearing a big round black hat and her long black hair was in a tight braided ponytail. She had huge dark sunglasses on and was smiling broadly as she got closer and closer. Her long muscular legs looked fabulous.

"You are even more gorgeous in person," she told me in that wonderfully husky voice as she bent forward to kiss one cheek and then the other.

"Oh Sam...You look gorgeous," I groaned my reply. It thrilled me to see all the heads turning as we made our way to the baggage claim to get her luggage. And even more when she reached down to hold my hand as we waited at the turnstile.

"Ha-ha-ha-ha, I should have guessed that you would have a Hummer," Sam giggled when I pointed out my forest green Humvee.

"It was my divorce present to myself," I informed her as I opened the passenger door. "And my cabin in the hills was the other." My dick wiggled as she swung her legs into the vehicle. I got a quick glance of her white panties and a great look down the top of her dress at her tits. Her nipples were just as hard as last night.

"I have something to tell you before we get to the hotel." She said it very softly as we were pulling out of the parking garage. "I make porn movies, Bobby...I am a porn Queen in Russia."

I glanced over at her and she was gazing at me intently. "Wow, Sam...How did I ever get so lucky?" My voice sort of trembled a bit. "I'm even more amazed that you have an interest in me now."

I felt her hand rest gently on my thigh as I turned my attention back to driving the vehicle. "I think that I may be the lucky one," she whispered it softly. "I came here to see you because there is something I need to show you." She said it so softly that I could barely hear her. "I have a feeling about you...that it will be okay." Her hand gently brushed up and down my thigh. I could feel my dick throbbing in my jeans. "You have no idea how much I hope I am right," she added.

I couldn't keep my eyes off of Sam while she was checking in at the hotel. Neither could any of the other men in the front lobby area. By the time we made it to the elevator, several of the bell hops and a couple of the men from the lobby had asked Sam for her autograph. Except they knew her by the name Samantha Bone.

I could tell that Sam was a bit annoyed and upset as the elevator started to rise towards the penthouse suite. "It bothers me that all those men knew who I am and have seen me naked," she whispered it softly. "But you haven't yet." She sort of hung her head as she finished.

I reached over and held her hand gently. "I'm sure that whatever you are worrying about will be okay," I told her as I squeezed her hand. "I've been told that I am a fairly progressive sort of man." I chuckled.

Sam turned to face me and gave me a half smile. "I certainly hope you are, Hun," she answered me.

As soon as were in the penthouse suite, Sam kicked off her white heels and tossed her black hat onto the easy chair near the kitchen. She sat her sunglasses on the counter then reached up to grab a bottle of vodka from the top cabinet.

"Oh Geezus," I gasped as I gazed at her ass sticking out under her tight dress as it pulled up in back.

Sam poured the vodka into two 4 oz. tumblers then carried them and the bottle back into the living room. "Sit on the couch and be comfortable," she told me as she handed me one of the drinks. After she slammed down her entire drink, she pointed to mine. "Bottoms up...Hun," she giggled. As soon as I swallowed mine down, she refilled both tumblers and then stepped back about two feet from the couch.

"Moment of truth," she chuckled softly. Standing directly in front of me, she slowly pulled down the top of her tight dress until her tits were fully exposed to me. "Oooh Sam," I gasped. I could feel my pecker swelling in my jeans as I glanced at her gorgeous tits.

"The reason I didn't tell you about the porn movies is that I was afraid that you might ask me what sort of porn." She said it as she wiggled her dress down to her feet and kicked it off. I could now see that she wasn't wearing white panties, it was a white bikini bottom.

"You are so gorgeous, Sam," I moaned as I gawked at her beautiful body.

"Yes...but you haven't seen all of me yet," she whispered as she pulled the strings on her bikini and it fell off.

What she had on underneath the bikini I had never seen before. It was like a thong. But not quite a thong. It was a small fabric cup sort of thing with a thong strap in the center that went up the crack of her ass. There was a thick string that wrapped around her waist and tied to the center fabric in back. "This is what you haven't seen," she said it timidly as she reached behind to untie the string.

As the tiny cup fell to the floor, I was stunned and exhilarated at the same instant. My eyes were riveted between her legs at the perfect six inch flaccid cock. "Ooooh Sam," I whispered. "That is so...extraordinary." I could feel my dick throbbing.

"It's....okay?" Sam cooed as her eyes lifted up to peer into mine.

"Oh Sam, it's better than okay...it is...wonderful! I want to feel it get hard in my hand this first time," I whispered as I reached forward to gently fondle her perfect six inch dick…

If you enjoyed this sample then look for **E-Mail Order Bride**.

BISEXUAL INTERRACIAL
EROTICA

JENNIFER'S
TOES
JUST PLAIN BOB

Martha and I made love that night, and when it was over and she was softly snoring beside me, I laid there looking up at the ceiling and wondering just what the hell was wrong with me. I had a loving wife who had been sexually satisfying me for twenty-eight years, so why was I risking it for a twenty-six-year-old unknown? Jennifer had a young, firm, well-toned body, but that didn't mean she was a good lay. Martha was not young, firm and well-toned; but she gave superb head, loved anal and was multi-orgasmic when I made love to her. I loved her and I didn't want to spend my life with anyone else but her, so what the hell was I doing? I saw Jennifer in my mind and I saw her wiggling her toes and I twitched down there. Shit! I rolled over on my side and tried to go to sleep.

***

Jennifer was sitting in her car when I pulled into the company lot on Monday. Before I had even turned off my ignition she got out of her car and hurried over to mine, got in and slid over next to me:

"Kiss me, lover; give the office gossips something to work with."

While we swapped tongues, her hand pulled down my zipper and she reached inside.

"Did you think about me all weekend, baby? All I thought about every hour was what we are going to do tomorrow, baby. Darnell told me that I could, lover; I've got the go ahead. You still want me, baby? My toes missed you, lover. Now that we have Darnell's permission, maybe you can get out of the house next Saturday or Sunday so we can spend some quality time together. Would you like that, lover? Oh shit, baby, put that away before I'm tempted to give you a blow job right here in the parking lot. We're going to be late, baby, tuck it away," and she slid out of the car and walked away leaving me with a case of blue balls.

All day I looked over at Jennifer and saw her smiling at me and she would glance down, and when I followed her glance, I would end up looking at her toes and I would twitch. I had it bad – I had it real bad.

About ten, Jennifer asked me to give her a hand getting something out of the supply room. We were no sooner in the door than she turned and kissed me. She ran her hand down my front until she got to it and began to squeeze it. She broke the kiss:

"God baby, I want you so bad. I don't want to wait until tomorrow, but I promised my sister I'd have lunch with her today."

She kissed me again, and just as I slipped my tongue into her mouth, the door opened and Maude from Accounting came in and saw us. "Oh excuse me," she said and she turned and left.

Jennifer giggled and said, "I was about two seconds from going to my knees and taking you in my mouth. The next twenty-four hours are going to drive me crazy, baby. I don't want to wait." She kissed me again and said, "We'd best get back to work before I pull you down and make you take me right here on the floor."

I didn't get a damned thing done that day. All I did was look at Jennifer and think about the next day.

***

I didn't get anything done the next morning either. I'd look at Jennifer and then at the clock and tried to will the time to pass quickly. Naturally, just the opposite happened. Seconds seemed like minutes and minutes seemed like hours. Finally lunchtime arrived and I was so keyed up that I pushed Jennifer away when she slid over next to me in the truck.

"If you touch me, I'll shoot in my pants. You have me so hot right now that it is all I can do to keep from pulling over to the side of the road and doing you right here in the daylight in front of God and everybody."

"I turn you on, baby?"

"Oh God yes."

"I have a surprise for you, baby. I'm so eager for this that I stopped and got the room on the way to work this morning so you wouldn't have to waste time checking in. Park outside room 121, baby."

If you enjoyed this sample then look for **Jennifer's Toes**.

STEAMY BI-SEXUAL EROTICA

EVERYTHING
I Wanted To Do

BY
SCOUT ALLEN

"Did you ever think we'd be doing this?" she asked as she pulled off her shirt and unbuckled her pants.

"Yeah but not without getting arrested," I commented while I slipped off my pants and pulled off my shirt.

We were in the country of Italy, Rome more specifically, at the fountain of Trevi. You know that large fountain with statues of horses and Italian people, large water out front and sprayers?

Anyway, I and my friend had been doing the whole backpacking through Europe thing when the Disappearance happened.

"Hey what are you doing?" I asked as she was pulling down her panties.

"What? If I'm going to go swimming in Rome's world famous Trevi fountain, I'm going to do it naked," then she pulled off her bra and looked at me. "Aren't you?"

Samantha wasn't a curvy goddess but she was pretty. Five foot six, B-cup breasts, bright red hair, blue eyes just bright enough to catch the eye, slim but not starvingly so, with slight hips that go down to a strip of hair leading to her otherwise bare sex. She was the most beautiful woman I'd seen in ages.

"Julian?" she said as I checked her out, her not shy in the least.

"Oh yeah," and I quickly stripped out of my shorts.

Climbing over the stone edge, we began our swimming around, thankfully because my penis had become erect.

"I wonder where they all went," she mused for what seemed like the hundredth time.

"Who knows," I added.

Not three days ago, the world seemed to have enough of the people's bullshit and it seemed like everyone else was just…gone. No clothing left over, no corpses to clean up, no crashes of cars. Time seemed to stop for everyone. And then when it was back, we were alone.

Thinking to myself, I wondered where everyone was, what they were doing, how we were missed in it all.

Something touched my skin and I fumbled and partially drowned myself before coming up for air. Sam was laughing out loud and standing on her feet, her bare breasts jiggling as she laughed.

I was now painfully erect.

"Why you.." and I tackled her back into the water as we wrestled and splashed until we ended up against one statue with my back pressed against the wall and her pressed against me.

We were both panting from the exertion. Her bare skin pressed against mine, her breasts pressed against my chest as she looked into my eyes. My painfully erect penis pressed against her warm crotch. Something came to mind but I decided not to say it. Instead, I simply moved my hands down to her ass and gripped it.

We'd been alone together for three days, no sex for weeks for either of us. We were young, horny, and willing.

I kissed her and she kissed me back.

Pulling her ass so her lips where pressed against my cock, her soft skin in my hands as her hands roamed over my chest and skin sending ripples of pleasure through my body. She was hungry, lustful… so was I…

If you enjoyed this sample then look for <u>Everything I Wanted To Do</u>.

www.ingramcontent.com/pod-product-compliance
Lightning Source LLC
Chambersburg PA
CBHW071339130626
46556CB00004B/1953